This Walker book belongs to:

....

....

....

D0186147

**EAST SUSSEX
SCHOOLS LIBRARY
SERVICE**

568408	
Askews & Holts	Oct-2014
JF	£6.99

For Norton Juster – you get the idea

First published in Great Britain in 2013 by Walker Books Ltd
87 Vauxhall Walk, London SE11 5HJ

This edition published 2014

2 4 6 8 10 9 7 5 3 1

© 2013 Mo Willems

First published in the United States 2013 by Balzer + Bray, an imprint of HarperCollins Children's Books.
British publication rights arranged with Sheldon Fogelman Agency, Inc.

The right of Mo Willems to be identified as author/illustrator of this work has been
asserted by him in accordance with the Copyright, Designs and Patents Act 1988

This book has been typeset in Silentina and Clarendon

Printed in China

All rights reserved. No part of this book may be reproduced, transmitted or stored in
an information retrieval system in any form or by any means, graphic, electronic or mechanical,
including photocopying, taping and recording, without prior written permission from the publisher.

British Library Cataloguing in Publication Data:
a catalogue record for this book is available from the British Library

ISBN 978-1-4063-5558-1
❖
www.walker.co.uk

Mo Willems

Presents

That Is NOT
a Good Idea!

WALKER BOOKS
AND SUBSIDIARIES
LONDON · BOSTON · SYDNEY · AUCKLAND

"What luck!"

"Dinner!"

"Excuse me.

Would you care

to go

for a stroll?"

"Hmm ...

sure!"

"That is NOT a good idea!"

"Would you care

to continue our walk

into the deep,

dark woods?"

"Sounds fun!"

"That is REALLY NOT a good idea!"

"Would you care

to visit my nearby

kitchen?"

"I would love to!"

"That is REALLY, REALLY, REALLY NOT a good idea!"

"Would you care

to boil some water

for soup?"

"Certainly.

I do love soup!"

"That is
REALLY,
REALLY,
REALLY
NOT
a good idea!"

"Would you care

to look at my soup?

A key ingredient

is missing."

"That is
REALLY,
REALLY,
REALLY,
REALLY
NOT
a good idea!"

"Oh –

a key ingredient

IS missing."

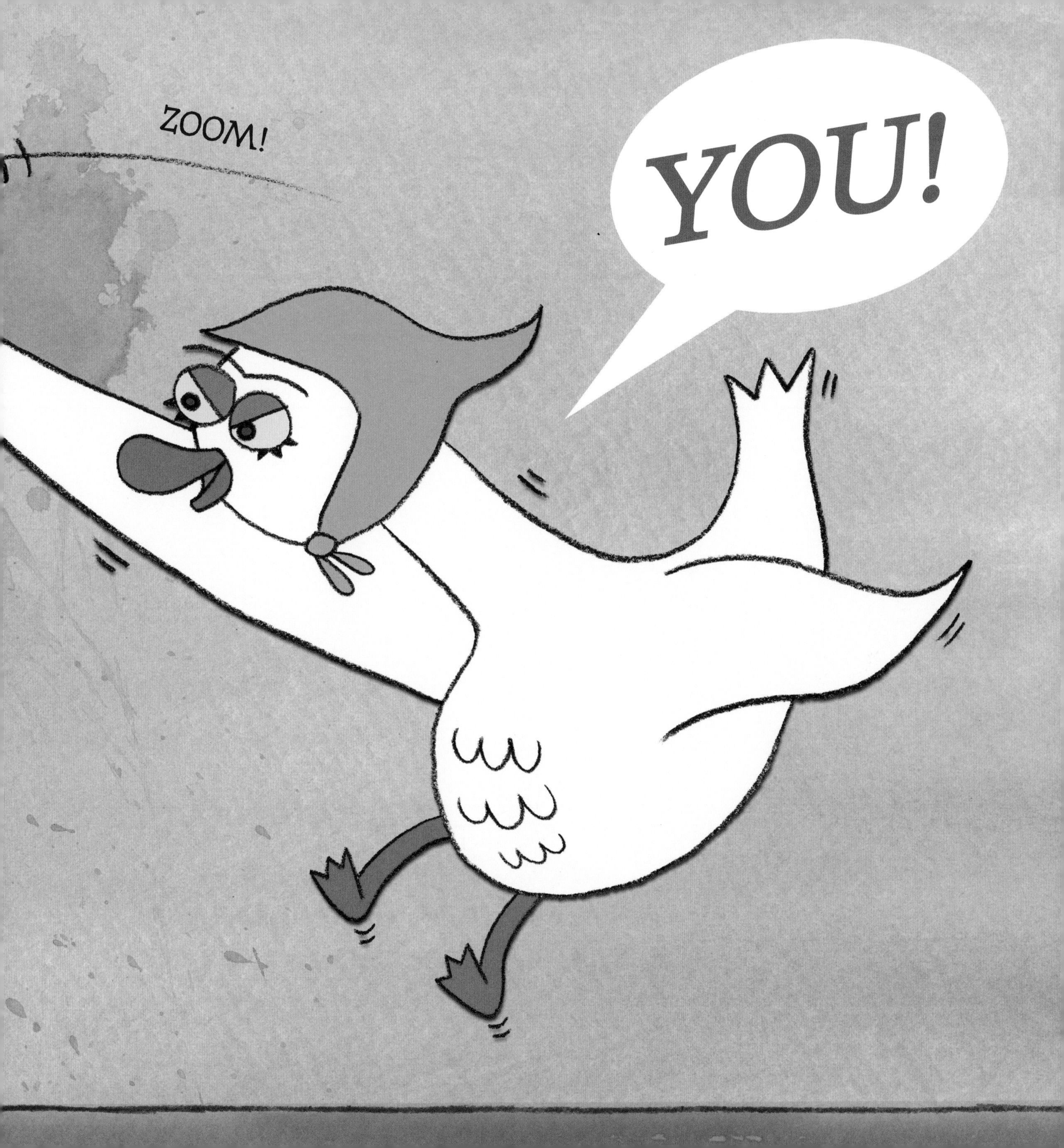
ZOOM!
YOU!

The END.

Mo Willems is the author of the Caldecott Honor-winning books
Don't Let the Pigeon Drive the Bus!, Knuffle Bunny and Knuffle Bunny Too
as well as Goldilocks and the Three Dinosaurs and the Theodor Seuss Geisel
Medal-winning Elephant and Piggie books. An acclaimed animator and television
script-writer, he has won six Emmy awards for his writing on Sesame Street and is also
the creator of Sheep in the Big City. Mo lives with his family in Massachusetts, USA.

Other books by Mo Willems:

ISBN 978-1-84428-513-6

ISBN 978-1-84428-545-7

ISBN 978-1-4063-0812-9

ISBN 978-1-4063-1550-9

ISBN 978-1-4063-4009-9

ISBN 978-1-4063-0158-8

ISBN 978-1-4063-1215-7

ISBN 978-1-4063-4731-9

ISBN 978-1-4063-1229-4

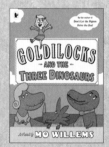
ISBN 978-1-4063-5532-1

ISBN 978-1-84428-059-9

ISBN 978-1-4063-1382-6

ISBN 978-1-4063-3649-8

ISBN 978-1-4063-2137-1

 Available from all good booksellers www.walker.co.uk